OLIVER
AND ALBERT,
FRIENDS
FOREVER

Jean Van Leeuwen

PICTURES BY

ANN SCHWENINGER

PHYLLIS FOGELMAN BOOKS
NEW YORK

For Thea Fry, a wonderful teacher

J.V.L.

For Sue Berkman

A.S.

Published by Phyllis Fogelman Books
An imprint of Penguin Putnam Books for Young Readers
345 Hudson Street
New York, New York 10014
Text copyright © 2000 by Jean Van Leeuwen
Pictures copyright © 2000 by Ann Schweninger
Printed in the U.S.A.

The Dial Easy-to-Read logo is a registered trademark of
Dial Books for Young Readers,
a division of Penguin Putnam Inc., ® TM 1,162,718.

1 3 5 7 9 10 8 6 4 2

Library of Congress Cataloging in Publication Data
Van Leeuwen, Jean.
Oliver and Albert, friends forever/Jean Van Leeuwen;
pictures by Ann Schweninger—1st ed.
p. cm.
Summary: Oliver makes friends with Albert,
the new boy in class, and they have fun together,
playing kickball and collecting bugs.
ISBN 0-8037-2517-5
[1. Pigs—Fiction. 2. Friendship—Fiction. 3. Schools—Fiction.]
I. Schweninger, Ann, ill. II. Title.
PZ7.V3273Olj   2000
[E]—DC21   99-27593   CIP   AC

Reading Level 1.9

The full-color artwork was prepared using carbon pencil,
colored pencils, and watercolor washes.

CONTENTS

THE NEW BOY

"We have a new boy in our class today,"

said Mrs. Theodora Pig.

"This is Albert."

Albert was tall.

"He is as big as a third grader,"
whispered Oliver to Bernard.
Albert raised his hand each time
Mrs. Theodora Pig asked a question.

"He knows everything,"
whispered Bernard to Oliver.
If Albert didn't know the answer,
he said, "I will look it up."

"He even knows how to read,"

whispered Oliver to Rosie.

Oliver and Rosie couldn't read yet.

But at recess they found out

something Albert couldn't do.

He could not play kickball.

He could not kick.

"*Oof!*" Albert missed the ball.

He could not catch.

"*Uh-oh!*" Albert dropped the ball.

And he could not run.

"*Oops!*" Albert fell over his own feet.

Oliver wished that Albert

was not on his team.

In the outfield they stood together.

Each time the ball came,

Albert cried, "I've got it!"

And each time, he didn't get it.

Once the ball bounced

right on his head.

Everyone laughed, even Albert.

But Oliver thought maybe

he was really crying.

Finally James was up.

"Watch out," Oliver told Albert.

"He is good."

James kicked the ball hard
and high and very far.

It was coming right at Albert.

But what was Albert doing?

He wasn't running after it.

He wasn't saying, "I've got it!"

He was just sitting in the grass

looking at something.

The ball rolled to the fence.

It was a home run.

"Hooray!" cheered the other team.

"What happened?" asked Oliver.

"Look," said Albert.

On the knee of his overalls

was a fuzzy caterpillar.

"Wow!" said Oliver.

"I love caterpillars."

"Me too," said Albert.

"It's called a woolly bear.

I looked it up."

"Can I hold it?" asked Oliver.

"Sure," said Albert.

Oliver and Albert sat in the outfield

looking at the caterpillar

until recess was over.

"That new boy Albert,"

whispered Bernard to Oliver.

"He can't kick and he can't catch."

"And he runs like a turkey," said James.

"I'm glad he wasn't on my team."

"Leave him alone," said Oliver.

"Albert is my friend."

PRACTICE

Albert was sad every day at recess.

"No one wants me

on their kickball team," he said.

"What you need is practice,"

said Oliver.

"Come to my house after school."

For their snack Mother put out
a plate of peanut butter cookies.
Albert ate six.

"Wow!" said Oliver.

"Now you will have power."

"Maybe I might even kick

a home run," said Albert.

Oliver rolled the ball.

Albert kicked so hard, he fell down.

Only he missed the ball.

"Keep your eye on the ball,"
said Oliver. "That is what
my father always tells me."
"I'll try," said Albert.

"And don't look for bugs," said Oliver.

Oliver rolled the ball.

Albert kicked.

"I did it!" he cried.

The ball went high in the air.

Only it came right down again

and Oliver caught it.

"Phooey," said Albert. "It's an out."

"Keep trying," said Oliver.

"Remember,

you have peanut butter power."

Albert kept trying.

Sometimes he still missed.

Sometimes he kicked the ball

high in the air

and Oliver didn't catch it.

"It's a hit!" said Albert. "A real hit!"

"Good one," said Oliver.

Finally Albert kicked a really good one.

It went over Oliver's head,

over the little pine tree,

over Oliver's sister, Amanda,

riding her bike in the driveway,

and into the next yard.

"Home run!" said Oliver.

"Hooray! I told you that

you had peanut butter power."

"I can't believe it," said Albert.

"A real home run!"

"Let's get a drink," said Oliver.

"Then we can practice catching."

They sat under the little pine tree

drinking lemonade.

Oliver felt something tickling him.

"Look," he said. "An anthill."

"I love ants," said Albert.

"They are so busy," said Oliver,

"but I don't know what they are doing."

Oliver and Albert lay in the grass
and watched the busy ants.

"Do you know what?" said Albert.

"What?" asked Oliver.

"Even if I have peanut butter power,"
Albert said,

"and even if I got a home run,

I still like bugs better than kickball."

A SPIDERWEB

Now in Mrs. Theodora Pig's room

there was a jar with a caterpillar

and a jar full of ants.

Soon Samantha brought in a ladybug.

James brought in a cricket.

"Wow!" said Oliver.

"It is a whole bug zoo."

"This can be our science table,"

said Mrs. Theodora Pig.

"It will be fun to watch our insects

and learn more about them."

One morning during reading

Oliver saw something on Rosie's chair.

"Look," he whispered to Albert.

"It's a spiderweb."

Albert whispered to Bernard.

Bernard whispered to James.

James whispered to Rosie.

"Oh!" said Rosie.

She jumped right out of her chair.

"What is the matter?"

asked Mrs. Theodora Pig.

"Rosie is scared of a little spider,"

said Bernard.

"I was not scared," said Rosie,

"just surprised."

"But now the spiderweb

is all wrecked," said Oliver.

Mrs. Theodora Pig lifted Rosie's chair
onto the science table.

"Oliver is right," she said.

"The web is broken.

But maybe if we watch carefully,

we will see the spider spin a new one."

They all watched carefully.

Nothing happened.

"Maybe the spider is asleep,"

said Bernard.

Then Albert said, "I see it!

It is starting to spin."

"How long does it take to make a web?"

asked Rosie.

"What kind of spider is it?"

asked Oliver.

"Those are good questions,"

said Mrs. Theodora Pig.

"How can we find out the answers?"

"I could go to the library," said Albert,

"and look it up."

"Me too," said Oliver.

"Good idea," said Mrs. Theodora Pig.

Oliver and Albert went to the library.

They found six books about spiders.

Oliver took three.

Albert took three.

It was very quiet in the library.

"Did you find anything?"

whispered Albert to Oliver.

"I don't know," whispered Oliver.

"I can't read."

"Oh," said Albert. "I forgot.

But never mind, I will help you."

So Oliver and Albert sat side by side

on the library floor.

And Albert read to Oliver

all about spiders.

THE FIGHT

"Let's look for more bugs,"

said Oliver at recess.

"Great!" said Albert.

So while everyone else was running

and jumping and climbing

and playing kickball,

Oliver and Albert looked for bugs.

"What is that thing," said Oliver,

"over there in the grass?"

"It's a grasshopper," said Albert.

"Oh, I love grasshoppers."

Quietly he crept through the grass.

He reached for the grasshopper.

"Got it!" he said.

But the grasshopper hopped away.

"Let me try," said Oliver.

He took off his baseball hat.

He wiggled like a worm

through the grass.

"Hello, little grasshopper," he said.

And he plopped his hat on top of it.

But the grasshopper hopped away.

"I have an idea," said Albert.

"I will chase the grasshopper to you,

and you catch it."

"Okay," said Oliver.

Albert bent down.

He reached for the grasshopper.

It hopped away toward Oliver.

Albert reached for it again.

It hopped again, closer to Oliver.

"Ready?" asked Albert.

"Ready," said Oliver.

The grasshopper hopped.

Oliver caught it right in his hat.

"Nice catch," said Albert.

They put some grass in the hat
in case the grasshopper was hungry.
"I will carry it to our room,"
said Oliver, "and show it
to Mrs. Theodora Pig."

"I should carry it," said Albert.

"It was my idea."

"But it is my hat," said Oliver.

Albert grabbed the hat.

"That's not fair!" he said.

"It is so!" said Oliver.

He grabbed it back.

The hat fell in the grass

and the grasshopper hopped away.

"Now look what you did," said Albert.

"Look what *you* did," said Oliver.

He scowled at Albert.

Albert scowled back.

Suddenly Oliver smiled.

"Don't move," he whispered.

"It's sitting on your foot."

Oliver caught the grasshopper

and put it back in the hat.

"Wow!" said Albert. "It must like us."

Together they carried it to their room.

Together they put it in a jar

on the science table.

"Something new for our bug zoo,"

said Mrs. Theodora Pig. "How exciting!"

"It was hard to catch," said Albert.

"But we helped each other," said Oliver.

He smiled at Albert.

Albert smiled back.

"Helping each other,"

said Mrs. Theodora Pig,

"is what friends do best."

"Yes," said Oliver and Albert together.

Oliver and Albert.

Friends forever.